A Farmer's Life for Me

Written by Jan Dobbins

Illustrated by Laura Huliska-Beith

Sung by The Flannery Brothers

Barefoot Books
Step inside a story

Up jump the farmers and set off on their way.

Up jump the children, ready for the day.

Off they go together and this is what they say:

1, 2, 3, it's a farmer's life for me.

It's time for the milking. The cow's named Annabelle.

Careful! She'll kick you and spill the milk as well.

We go up to the henhouse, running all the way.

How many warm eggs will we find today?

Pick them up carefully and put them in the tray.

1, 2, 3, it's a farmer's life for me.

Out in the orchard, there blows a summer breeze.
Fat, red cherries are ripening on the trees.

Would you like to eat some? *Mmm!* Yes, please!

1, 2, 3, it's a farmer's life for me.

We're down at the pigsty, peeping through the door
At one mother pig and her family of four.
Can you see the piglets drinking more and more?
1, 2, 3, it's a farmer's life for me.

Over in the meadow, the farmer mows the hay.

Soon it will be dry on this lovely sunny day.

Rake it and turn it,
the baler's on its way.
1, 2, 3, it's a farmer's life for me.

Up on the hillside, we're counting lambs and sheep.

Some lambs are lost, though we can hear them bleat.

Rattle the bucket and give them all a treat.

1, 2, 3, it's a farmer's life for me.

Down in the paddock, we check the water trough.

The horses are thirsty; have they got enough?

Turn on the hosepipe. *Whoosh!* Now turn it off.

1, 2, 3, it's a farmer's life for me.

Back in the farmhouse, it's time to make a cake.

Let's get ready so we can start to bake.

Leave it to cool, then slice it into eight.

1, 2, 3, it's a farmer's life for me.

It's time to:

Feed all the ponies and shut the paddock gate.

Close up the henhouse before it gets too late.

The pigs are in the pigsty,

the mower's in the shed.

Work's done for the day, and now it's time for bed.

Work's done for the day, and now it's time for bed.

The Working Farm

There are farms all over the world. They are busy places where all sorts of people work to grow food and raise animals. It takes hard work to keep a farm in order. There are different animals to feed and care for, and lots of crops to grow. Some farmers use chemical fertilizers and sprays to help them grow as much food as they can. This is called intensive farming. When farmers use traditional farming methods that are free of chemicals, and let their animals live outside, this is called organic farming.

Milk

Cows, goats and other animals are raised primarily for their milk and meat. When a cow has been milked, the milk is pasteurized, which means it is scalded and strained to make it last longer and to make it safe for drinking and cooking. Milk is full of nutrients like calcium, protein and vitamin D. Dairy foods, such as cheese, butter, yogurt and ice cream, are all made from milk.

Eggs

Many farmers raise chickens, both for their meat and for their eggs. Battery-raised chickens are kept in barns without ever seeing the outdoors or being released from cages. Free-range chickens are allowed to graze outside, stretch their legs and enjoy the fresh air. Eggs are used in all kinds of recipes as well as being delicious on their own.

Cherries

Cherries are a kind of fruit. They are small and round and are grown by farmers in orchards. They are picked when they are juicy and ripe. Some cherries are sour and are used to make pies, jams, juices and smoothies. Other cherries are sweet enough to eat fresh.

Pigs

Pigs are raised by farmers for their meat. Bacon, sausages and pork all come from pigs. Pigskin is used for clothing, bags and horses' saddles.

Hay

In the summer months, many animals eat only grasses. However, in winter they need additional food, like hay. Hay meadows are made up of many different kinds of grasses and wild flowers. Farmers mow their hay meadows once or twice each summer, spread out the hay to dry, then gather it into bales and store it. Hay smells sweet and fragrant!

Sheep

Sheep have thick, woolly coats. In the spring, farmers shear their sheep, clipping off their thick winter wool. The shorn wool is then washed, combed and spun into yarn to make blankets and clothes, or the wool is used to insulate houses. Sheep and lambs are also raised for their meat.

Horses

Before farmers started using tractors and other large machines to do the hard work around the farm, they would use horses to till the fields, and to draw heavy loads by pulling carts and wagons. Nowadays, farmers sometimes use horses to round up cattle and sheep. They also ride them just for pleasure.

A Farmer's Life for Me

Light Fun Swing ♩ = 140

Up jump the farm-ers and set off on their way. Up jump the child-ren, read-y for the day.

Off they go to-geth-er and this is what they say: 1, 2, 3, it's a farm-er's life for me.

Barefoot Books • 2067 Massachusetts Ave • Cambridge, MA 02140
Barefoot Books • 29/30 Fitzroy Square • London, W1T 6LQ

Text and song copyright © 2013 by Jan Dobbins
Illustrations copyright © 2013 by Laura Huliska-Beith
Musical arrangement copyright © 2013 by The Flannery Brothers
The moral rights of Jan Dobbins and Laura Huliska-Beith have been asserted
Music performed by Mike and Dan Flannery with violins by Jacob Lawson
Recorded, mixed and mastered by Mike Flannery, New York City
Animation by Karrot Animation, London

First published in the United States of America by Barefoot Books, Inc
and in Great Britain by Barefoot Books, Ltd in 2013
All rights reserved

Graphic design by Katie Jennings, Nashville, TN
Reproduction by B & P International, Hong Kong
Printed in China on 100% acid-free paper
This book was typeset in Futura T and Spud AF Crisp
The illustrations were painted in gouache and acrylic
on Arches paper, and then digitally collaged

ISBN 978-1-84686-791-0

British Cataloguing-in-Publication Data:
a catalogue record for this book is available from the British Library
Library of Congress Cataloging-in-Publication Data
is available under LCCN 2012014538

9 8

Go to *www.barefootbooks.com/farmerslife* to access
your audio singalong and video animation online.